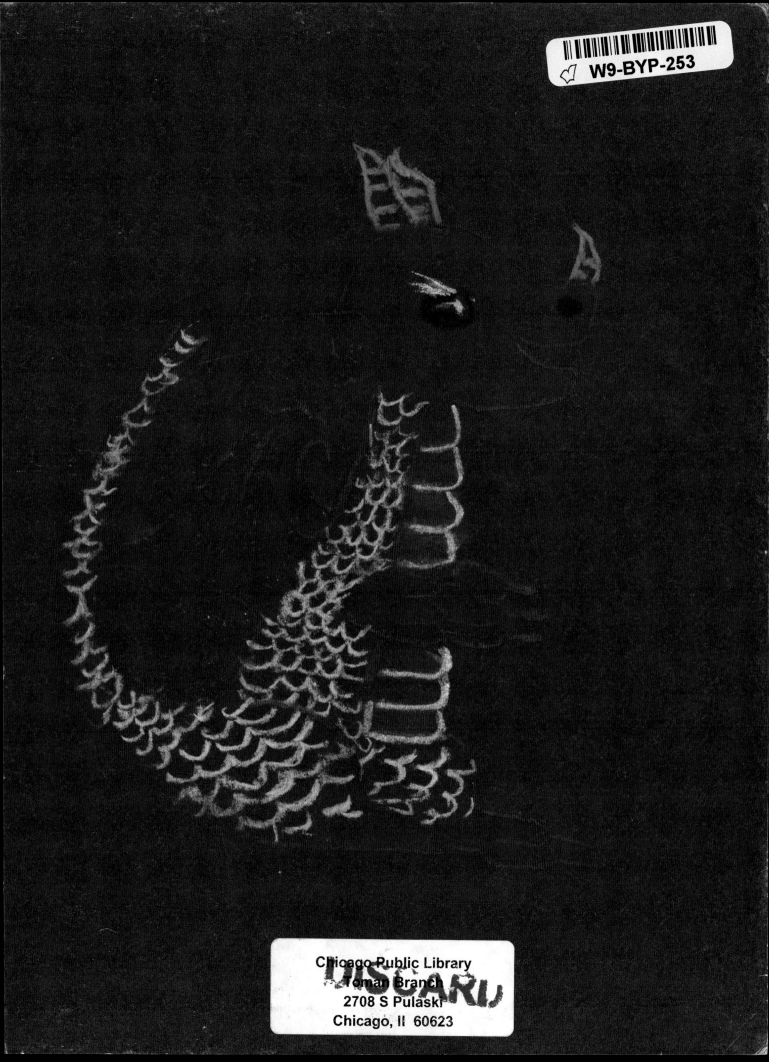

Front endpapers by Katherine Guo, aged 10
Back endpapers by Fabienne Derk, aged 10

Thank you to The Western Academy, Beijing, for helping
with the endpapers and for the wonderful week in China —K.P.

For Jenny and Louise in Canada —V.T.
For Sue Matthew —K.P.

Winnie's Midnight Dragon

Text copyright © 2006 by Valerie Thomas

Illustrations copyright © 2006 by Korky Paul

A hardcover edition of this book was first published in the
United Kingdom by Oxford University Press in 2006.

Printed in Singapore.

www.harpercollinschildrens.com

Library of Congress Catalog Card Number: 2007928021

ISBN 978-0-06-117314-1 (trade bdg.)

Typography by Rachel Zegar
1 2 3 4 5 6 7 8 9 10
❖
First HarperCollins Edition, 2008

www.korkypaul.com

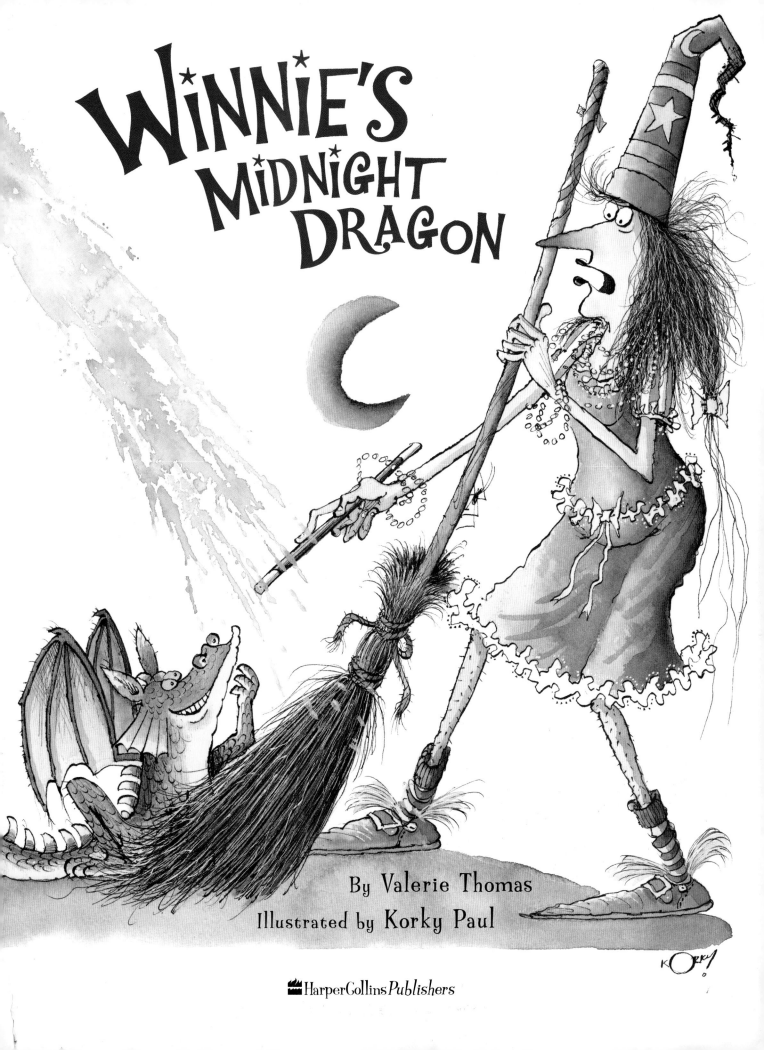

WINNIE'S MIDNIGHT DRAGON

By Valerie Thomas

Illustrated by Korky Paul

HarperCollins Publishers

"Time for bed," said Winnie the Witch, as the clock struck twelve. Witches always go to bed at midnight. Winnie turned off the lights and went upstairs.

She brushed her teeth, washed her face, put on her nightie and climbed into bed. In two minutes she was snoring.

Wilbur, her big black cat, was already asleep.
He was curled up in his basket, dreaming.

Two minutes later, Wilbur woke up. He could hear a funny noise in the garden.

He crept to the cat flap and peeped out. There was something on the doormat. Something with big green eyes.

"Meeoww!" cried Wilbur, and he jumped back. A long nose poked through the cat flap.

Then there was a puff of smoke. The cat flap wobbled and shook.

A spiky body, then a long tail, followed the nose.
There was a baby dragon in Winnie's house!
"Meeoww!" cried Wilbur. He turned three
backward somersaults and ran into the hall.

The baby dragon thought this was fun.
He ran after Wilbur. *Swish, swish* went his tail.
Winnie's grandfather clock wobbled and shook.

DING! DONG! BOING!

"Meeoww!" cried Wilbur, and he raced upstairs.
The baby dragon ran after him. *Swish, swish*
went his tail. Winnie's suit of armor wobbled
and shook and rolled down the stairs.

CRASH! BANG! CLANG!

"Meeoww!" cried Wilbur outside Winnie's door. Winnie woke up and jumped out of bed. "Whatever's that?" she said.

Then she saw a puff of smoke coming from behind her broomstick. "Oh no!" said Winnie. "My broomstick is on fire!"

Winnie grabbed her broomstick. "Goodness gracious me!" said Winnie. "It's a baby dragon! He could burn my house down. We'll have to find his mother, Wilbur."

"Where's your mother,
little dragon?" Winnie asked.
"Boo hoo hoo," cried the baby dragon.

A cloud of smoke came out
of his nose. *Puff, puff.*

Then Winnie had an idea. She waved
her magic wand three times and shouted,

ABRACADABRA!

"Puff!" went the dragon,
and out of his nose came . . .

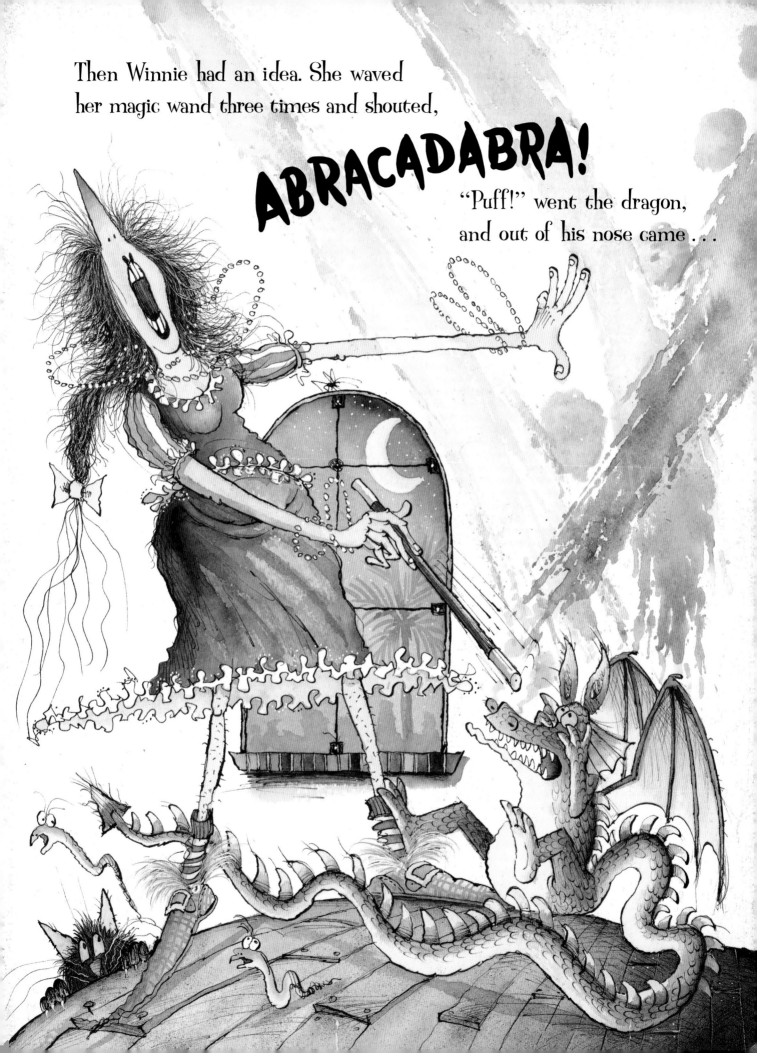

a cloud of butterflies.
"Puff, puff, puff," went the baby dragon,
who was very surprised.

SMASH!
went Winnie's best bowl.

SPLASH!
went the vase of flowers.

There were butterflies everywhere.
Wilbur loved chasing butterflies.
The baby dragon loved chasing anything!

CRASH!
went the table.

"That wasn't such a good idea," said Winnie.
She waved her magic wand again
and shouted,

ABRACADABRA!

Out of the dragon's nose came . . .
nothing.

"Good," said Winnie. "Now let's get some sleep."
But the baby dragon didn't want to sleep.
He wanted to play.

"Bother!" said Winnie.
"We'd better find your mother right now!"

She got a flashlight and went out onto the roof.
"Yoo-hoo," she called.

It was quiet and dark on the roof.
"Yoo-hoo," Winnie called again and
waved her flashlight.

Suddenly there was a flash of fire,
and the sound of great wings.
The baby dragon jumped up and down.
"Mamamamama," he called.
"Yoo-hoo-hoo!" called Winnie.

But the baby dragon's mother didn't see them.
Then Winnie had a wonderful idea.

She grabbed her wand,
waved it six times, shouted,

ABRACADABRA!

and there, above her house,

was an enormous moon.

The mother dragon came flying back.
She swooped down and scooped up her baby.

"Wait a minute!" called Winnie.
She waved her magic wand and shouted,

ABRACADABRA!

"Puff!" went the baby dragon, and smoke
came out of his nose again.

The two dragons flew high into the sky and disappeared.

Winnie waved her wand, shouted,

ABRACADABRA!

and the enormous moon went out.
"Now let's go back to bed, Wilbur," she said.

Winnie climbed into bed and shut her eyes.
In half a minute she was snoring.
Wilbur was already asleep in his basket.

Just then, the sun rose. The night was over.
But Winnie the Witch and Wilbur were fast asleep.